WELCOME to CAMP PIKACHU

Unofficial Stories for Pokémon Collectors

WELCOME to CAMP PIKACHU

Unofficial Stories for Pokémon Collectors

ALEX POLAN

Sky Pony Press
New York

Copyright © 2016 by Hollan Publishing, Inc.

First Edition

This is a work of fiction. Names, characters, places, and incidents are
either products of the author's imagination or used fictitiously.

Sky Pony Press books may be purchased in bulk at special discounts for
sales promotion, corporate gifts, fund-raising, or educational purposes.
Special editions can also be created to specifications. For details, contact
the Special Sales Department, Sky Pony Press, 307 West 36th Street,
11th Floor, New York, NY 10018 or info@skyhorsepublishing.com.

Sky Pony® is a registered trademark of Skyhorse Publishing, Inc.®,
a Delaware corporation.

Visit our website at www.skyponypress.com.

10 9 8 7 6 5 4 3 2 1

Library of Congress Cataloging-in-Publication Data is available on file.

Special thanks to Erin L. Falligant.

Cover illustration by Matt Armstrong
Cover design by Sarah Brody

Print ISBN: 978-1-5107-0378-0
Ebook ISBN: 978-1-5107-0379-7

Printed in Canada

CHAPTER ONE

"**P**ika, Pika," chirped Pikachu from his place on Marco's shoulder.

"I know," said Marco, wading through the tall grass. "We should have found a secret base by now."

He shaded his eyes and spun in a circle to search the trees beyond the clearing. "We have to capture a flag. We can't let Team Treecko down."

"Pi-ka," agreed Pikachu.

Suddenly, a low growl sounded from the woods. Marco dropped to his knees.

"Did you hear that?" he whispered.

"Pik-a-CHU!" said his Pokémon friend. Pikachu was always ready for a battle.

Marco's legs shook as he stood to meet their opponent. A wild Mightyena stepped out of the woods with drool dripping from his sharp fangs. As his red eyes locked on to Pikachu, he flattened his silver-gray back and growled.

Marco fought the urge to turn and run. Pikachu needed him. He needed a command from his Trainer.

"Pikachu, do a Tail Whip!" said Marco, his voice cracking.

Pikachu leaped at the Mightyena, smacking him off his feet with his lightning-bolt tail.

But the Mightyena sprang up and lunged at Pikachu. Its sharp teeth clamped down on the Pokémon's tail.

Pikachu cried out and tried to wrestle free.

"Thunder Shock!" called Marco. "Do Thunder Shock!"

Before Pikachu could attack, they heard another high-pitched howl. Then more Mightyena—many more—stepped out from the trees.

Five, six, seven . . . Marco tried to count them all. "Pikachu, retreat!" he called. His friend was at his feet in an instant. They turned and ran.

Marco heard the snapping and growling of the Mightyena on his heels. He felt their hot breath. Suddenly, something grabbed his leg and yanked him backward, pulling him down, down, down. . . .

"Yeow!" screamed Marco, shaking free—from Logan's grip. He tumbled off the bed and fell with a *thump* onto the cabin floor.

"Whoa, sorry!" said Logan, peering over the edge of the bed. "I was trying to wake you up." He was already dressed, but his sandy brown hair was still messy from sleep. "What were you dreaming about?"

Marco rubbed his eyes. "We were playing capture the flag, but I couldn't find a single crummy flag." He didn't tell Logan about the Mightyena. Not just yet. His heart was still pounding from that part of the dream.

Logan laughed. "That's crazy talk," he said. "Team Treecko is going to capture a bunch of flags today—I already know it." He jumped up and ran a victory lap around the tiny cabin. "And, in first place, after capturing a gazillion and one flags, Team Treecko!" he shouted, pumping his fists in the air.

Marco shook his head. Even early in the morning, Logan had more energy than anyone he knew. And he was crazy about Pokémon just like Marco. That's how they both ended up at Camp Pikachu, a summer camp where kids got to act out Pokémon adventures. It was only week two, but Marco felt as if he'd known Logan forever.

"We don't have to capture *every* flag," he reminded Logan. "We just have to get more than Team Fennekin."

Logan grimaced at the mention of the team that had beaten them in last week's challenge. Then he started jogging around the room again. "Let's hear it for Team Treecko, who clobbered Team Fennekin to get into this year's Camp Hall of Fame!"

Marco could see it already—his team winning the Poké Ball statue and getting their picture displayed in the glass case for future campers to see. But they would have to start winning competitions, beginning with capture the flag. And what if they couldn't find any flags?

His dream had felt so real. As Marco changed into his shorts and Team Treecko T-shirt, he checked his leg for bite marks. "I didn't find any flags in my dream," he said, "but a whole pack of Mightyena found me."

"Awesome!" said Logan, flopping back down on his bed. "Did you battle them?"

Marco shrugged. He knew Logan would have battled the Mightyena—and probably won. Logan was a year younger than Marco, but he wasn't afraid of anything.

"Pikachu and I tried, but . . . I mean, we were kind of outnumbered," said Marco, shivering at the memory. "I wish you'd been there. Which Pokémon would you have used?"

Logan climbed onto all fours. "I would have battled them myself," he said, pretending to wrestle an imaginary Mightyena. "Pokémon have way more fun than Trainers do."

Marco laughed. "If you were a Pokémon, I know what type you'd be. You'd definitely be a Grass one—like Treecko." Logan's knees were usually grass-stained. Plus, he climbed trees as well as their team mascot, a wood-gecko Pokémon.

"Treecko, Treecko, Treecko, Tree!" joked Logan in his best gecko voice. "What type would you be?"

Marco ran a hand over his dark, cropped hair. "I don't know," he said. Before he could answer, he heard a quick rap on the cabin door.

"The girls are here!" said Logan, jumping up.

Maddy stood on the step with a tray of Poké Puffs, which, at Camp Pikachu, was a fancy name for cupcakes. The tray looked way too heavy for such a small girl. Marco still couldn't believe Maddy was old enough to be at Camp Pikachu. She looked like she was only five or six, but she was actually seven. *Seven-and-a-half,* Marco corrected himself. At least that's what Maddy kept telling him.

Maddy blew her dirty-blonde bangs off her forehead and asked, "Who wants a Poké Puff? They're fresh from Professor Sycamore's lab."

Nisha stepped up beside her. "It's not a lab, Maddy," she said. "It's a kitchen." Nisha was a couple years older than Maddy and was already acting like a big sister.

Maddy furrowed her brow. "Professor Sycamore wears a white coat, and we mix things together like scientists. It is *too* a lab."

"Whatever," said Marco. "Who cares where they came from? Yum." He reached for a pink-frosted Poké Puff.

"Wait," said Maddy, pulling back the tray so it was out of his reach. "Logan, do you want to pick one first?" she asked sweetly.

Logan flushed a thousand shades of red. "Um, no thanks." He took a step backward.

Marco tried not to laugh. It was only the second week of camp, but Maddy already had a huge crush on Logan. And the sweeter she was to him, the saltier he was toward her. Logan was eyeing the cupcakes like they were mud cakes—worms and all.

Marco reached again for a Poké Puff, and this time Maddy let him have one. *If Maddy were a Pokémon, she'd be a Fairy-type,* he thought, taking his first bite. Her favorite Pokémon was Swirlix, the Fairy-type who looked like cotton candy. Maddy had a huge sweet tooth, and she always shared her treats.

As Nisha reached for a Poké Puff, Marco noticed the Band-Aid on her finger. "How did you hurt yourself?" he asked, pointing toward her hand.

"She's been biting her nails," Maddy reported.

Almost everything about Nisha was sharp and tidy. Her hair was smoothed back into a sleek, dark ponytail. Her lime-green Team Treecko T-shirt was tucked neatly into her shorts. But her fingernails? They were usually chewed to ragged little stubs.

Nisha shrugged. "Biting my nails helps me think. And I've been thinking a lot, trying to come up with good gear for our game today."

"Clemontic Gear?" asked Logan. "Like in the Pokémon cartoons?"

Marco laughed. In the cartoons, Ash's friend Clemont was really smart, but his inventions were always breaking down or blowing up.

"Better than Clemontic Gear," said Nisha. "Clemont's inventions don't usually work. Mine will."

"Does that mean you came up with a good idea?" asked Maddy, wiping frosting off her chin.

Nisha nodded, her eyes flashing.

"Well, where is it?" asked Logan. He looked her up and down as if she were hiding the gear in her pockets.

"Shh," whispered Nisha, glancing at the cabin behind her. "It's at our secret base. C'mon, I'll show you."

Maddy started to follow, but the tray of Poké Puffs wobbled in her hands. "Wait!" she said. "This is too heavy. I need something to put these in."

Marco searched the cabin, his eyes landing on a shoebox on his desk. "You can use this," he said. "It had cookies in it from home." *They sure didn't last long,* he thought, shaking the crumbs out of the bottom.

Maddy started to carry the tray into the cabin, but Logan held up a hand. "No girls allowed in boys' cabins." No boys were allowed in girls' cabins, either. Those were Camp Pikachu's rules, not Logan's. But Marco noticed that Logan was pretty quick to enforce them, especially where Maddy was concerned.

"I'll take them," Marco said, reaching for the tray.

After he had tucked the last cupcake into the box, Nisha led Team Treecko toward the woods. They walked past the other boys' cabins, which were clustered around the counselors' cabin, and then past the Dining Hall. As Nisha turned around to check on her friends, she nibbled nervously on a nail.

"Hey, maybe you could invent a way to stop chewing your fingernails," suggested Logan.

Everyone laughed—except Nisha. She had her game face on.

She's already thinking about ways to win capture the flag, thought Marco. He wished he had a big idea of his own. How could he make sure to capture a flag or two? His mind went blank. *No ideas here. Zip. Zero. Nada.*

As the group stepped onto the wooded trail, tall grass brushed against Marco's leg. He suddenly remembered his nightmare and whirled around to search the bushes for Mightyena.

Don't be a scaredy cat! he scolded himself. *That was just a dream.* There weren't any Mightyena in these woods. But the other part of the dream? That part could still come true. He might not capture any flags today.

Again, Marco wondered, *Am I going to let my new friends down?*

His stomach twisted as he followed them toward the secret base.

CHAPTER TWO

It's just like Fortree City, thought Marco as he followed Logan up the ladder to the tree house. The smooth boards were chocolate brown like the tree houses in the Pokémon videogame. And the short ladder led to a deck with a railing wrapped all the way around.

Marco ducked his head to follow Logan through the door to their secret base.

"Hey, the counselors delivered our water balloons!" Logan shouted, hurrying over to a tub of brightly colored balloons. Every team was supposed to get some to defend its base during capture the flag.

"Our flag's here, too," said Marco, pointing toward the lime-green banner in the corner. He carefully unrolled it to reveal Treecko, the gecko-like Pokémon, in a fighting pose.

"Should we hang it outside?" asked Logan eagerly.

"No, not yet," said Nisha as she stepped into the tree house. "We're supposed to wait till the game starts."

Logan's shoulders sank. He flopped down onto one of the Poké Ball cushions. Then he sat straight up again as if he'd remembered something important. "Where's your invention, Nisha?"

"Don't show it yet! Wait for me," called Maddy, out of breath as she hurried into the tree house clutching her cupcake box. She was the only member of Team Treecko who didn't have to duck.

When everyone was sitting down, Nisha reached behind the blackboard, which was propped up against the wall. She proudly pulled out a dirty orange life vest.

"Ta-da!" she said.

Maddy cocked her head like a curious puppy, but Logan looked disappointed. He sank back down onto his cushion.

Marco tried to be nice. "That's, um, really, um . . . wow."

"Wait for it . . ." said Nisha. Then she did something amazing. She reached into the life vest and pulled out an orange water balloon. And then a red one. And then a blue one. "It's a Balloon Vest!" she announced. The whole vest was filled with bright, squishy water balloons.

"Cool!" said Maddy. "But, wait, how did you make it? Did you cut that vest open?"

"No," said Nisha. "I went to the boathouse and found some that were already torn. I took the foam out and put balloons in. You can't see the balloons from the outside, can you?"

"No," said Logan, "but other teams will sure be able to see us in bright orange vests."

"He's right," said Marco. "They'll spot us from a mile away."

Nisha held up her hand like a stop sign. Then she reached behind the blackboard again. The next vest she pulled out was printed in camouflage colors: green, tan, and brown.

Logan's eyes lit up. "Okay, yeah," he said. "That one is cool."

"Then you can wear this Balloon Vest," said Nisha, smiling. "At least one of us will be hidden."

"Are there more?" asked Maddy, jumping up to peek behind the blackboard. Suddenly, she shrieked and fell backward.

"What?" asked Nisha, nearly dropping her Balloon Vest. "What did you see?"

Maddy started to laugh. "A mouse. Just an itty-bitty brown mouse. He scared me, though."

"Let me see!" said Logan.

Marco hung back, shivering a little. *How many other mice are living in here?* he wondered. He eyed the shadowy corners of the tree house.

But Maddy didn't seem scared of the mouse anymore. In fact, she was worried about him. "Don't hurt him, Logan!" she said. She got on her hands and knees and watched as Logan tilted the blackboard forward. Then she smiled.

"Come see, Marco," said Logan, waving him over.

So, Marco tiptoed up behind Maddy and glanced over her shoulder. The mouse was standing on his hind legs, sniffing the air. *He* is *pretty cute*, Marco had to admit.

But as the mouse dropped to all fours and wobbled toward the wall, Marco noticed he was dragging one of his feet.

"Oh, he's injured!" said Maddy. "No wonder he's not running away." Then she kicked into full Fairy-type mode. "Nisha, hand me that box," she ordered.

Nisha wrinkled her nose. "You're going to put him in the Poké Puff box? Eww."

Maddy nodded like it was the most logical idea in the world.

"But . . . what are we going to do with the Poké Puffs?" asked Nisha.

Maddy shrugged. "Eat them, I guess."

No one argued. Soon, the little brown mouse was tucked into the box with a soft blanket—one of Maddy's socks. She struggled to get her bare foot back into her shoe. Then she reached out her hand so the mouse could sniff her fingers. He nibbled at the end of her braided friendship bracelet.

"I'll bet he's hungry," she said. "I'll have to bring him some food. What do mice eat?"

"Wait, you're keeping him here?" asked Marco. "Maybe he would be safer in your cabin."

Nisha glanced up, alarmed. "Or . . . maybe you could bring him to the Health Center," she said quickly. Nisha shared a cabin with Maddy, but she clearly wasn't a big fan of mice.

"No, living out here is better," said Logan. "He will feel like he's still outside. He'll be happier." Glancing out the tree house window, Logan looked pretty content, too.

"Yes!" said Maddy. "Mr. Mouse will be happier out here." She smiled up at Logan like he was her hero—or her Prince Charming.

Logan suddenly looked a lot less happy. He scooted his Poké Ball cushion an inch in the other direction.

When Maddy opened her mouth to say something, a sneeze came out instead.

"Uh-oh," said Nisha. "Are you allergic to mice?"

Maddy wrinkled her forehead. "I don't think so. I'm allergic to cats, though."

That's when they heard the low yeowl coming from the deck outside.

Marco and Logan locked eyes. "Meowth," Marco muttered under his breath. Both boys jumped up and headed for the door.

The yellow tomcat was prowling the deck. He turned and stared at them through narrowed eyes. Then he let out another yeowl and flicked his crooked tail before disappearing around the corner.

"Meowth!" called a voice from below. "Here, kitty, kitty . . ."

Marco glanced at Logan and raised a finger to his lips. They had to be quiet, or they'd give away the location of their secret base.

When Marco flattened himself onto his belly and peeked over the edge of the deck, he instantly saw the fox-orange T-shirts.

Team Fennekin.

There was Sam's spiky orange hair and freckled face. He was searching the bushes for Meowth. And wherever Sam was, his older sister, Stella, wasn't far behind.

Like Fennekin, their fox-like team mascot, Sam and Stella seemed sneaky—even downright mean. On the first day of camp, Sam had put a cricket in Maddy's lemonade and made her cry. She wasn't upset because her drink was ruined. She was worried the cricket would drown.

And now that he knew he could make her cry, Sam had been teasing her ever since.

"Who's there?" asked Maddy loudly, stepping onto the deck.

"Shh!" Marco heard Logan whisper.

Too late. Sam caught sight of Maddy.

"Well, if it isn't Maddy Waddy and Team Treecko," he said in a snide voice. "Or should I say Team Tickle-Tickle-Tickle. Wook at da widdle baby on da deck."

Stella stepped up behind him and glanced upward. She was tall and wore her hair in a sharp bob with magenta streaks. *She can't be only ten,* thought Marco. She looked like a teenager.

Sam, on the other hand, was small for his age. But he sure had a big mouth.

"Tickle, Tickle, Tickle," he said again. "Cootchie-coo. Oh, is da widdle baby going to cry?"

Marco swung his head around to look at Maddy. Her cheeks were blotchy and her hands were clenched into fists.

He had to do something—quick. But before he could think of anything, Sam jumped back. "Ouch!" he cried, rubbing his head.

"What happened?" asked Stella. "What are you blubbering about?"

Sam looked up nervously. "I don't know," he said. "I think someone threw something at me."

Stella narrowed her eyes and glanced up through the branches. *Does she see me?* wondered Marco, holding his breath. It looked like she was staring right through him with her chilly gaze.

After a few seconds, she smirked and said, "Looks like you got beat up by da widdle baby, Sammy." She laughed sharply and walked away, leaving Sam behind. He stared up for another few seconds, and then he turned and raced after his sister.

When the coast was clear, Marco got to his knees. "What happened?" he asked Logan.

Logan grinned and held out his fists. "Walnuts," he said proudly. "Walnuts happened." He uncurled his fingers to reveal two bumpy green pods.

"Walnuts?" asked Marco, reaching out to take one of the green balls. "I wish I'd thought of that."

He smiled as he followed Logan back into the tree house. Team Treecko had already scored one for the day. And capture the flag hadn't even begun.

CHAPTER THREE

"I'm *not* a little baby," said Maddy, still fighting back tears. "I'm seven—and a half."

"I know," said Nisha. "Don't worry about what Sam says. Just ignore him."

Logan looked like he was chewing on a thought— something he wasn't sure he should say out loud. "You may not be a little kid," he finally blurted, "but you do have a Dedenne like Bonnie has."

"A what?" asked Marco.

"A Dedenne—the Pokémon that Clemont's little sister, Bonnie, takes care of," Logan explained.

"It's a Fairy-type," Nisha said to Maddy. "Well, part Electric and part Fairy. You'd like him." Nisha knew all the Pokémon types. Marco wondered if she had the whole Pokédex memorized.

Maddy perked up. "That's a good name. I'll call my mouse Dedenne." Then she shot Logan one of her adoring glances. "Thanks, Logan," she said. "You always make me feel better."

Logan gave an exasperated sigh. As he pushed past Marco, he muttered, "I think I'll go throw up."

"What?" asked Maddy.

Logan stopped in his tracks. "I said . . . um . . ." He looked at Marco for help.

"He said, um, that he thinks he'll go blow up . . . a few more water balloons," said Marco.

Maddy cocked her head like she didn't quite believe him. But then a loud *thweet* cut through the air.

"That's Professor's Birch's whistle!" said Nisha, re-tucking her T-shirt into her shorts. "We have to get back to camp. It's time to start the game."

Team Treecko carefully climbed down the tree house ladder and hurried back along the path. When they reached the edge of the woods, most of the other teams were already there.

Team Torchic sat on the ground, bright as sunshine in their yellow tees. Marco recognized the Pokémon on their shirts right away—it looked like a baby chick. Team Mudkip wore blue tees, the color of their fish-like mascot. And Team Froakie, wearing aqua, hopped in like a bunch of long-legged frogs.

"Which team is that again?" asked Marco, nudging Logan. He pointed to the kids wearing chestnut-brown tees.

Nisha answered first. "That's Team Chespin," she said. "Chespin is that little spiny-nut Pokémon."

Marco nodded like he understood, but he didn't really. How could a Pokémon be both an animal and a nut? Then he realized that one of the teams was missing. Where was Team Fennekin?

They're sneaking around here somewhere, thought Marco. *Probably in a fox den under the ground.*

There! Stella and Sam, in their orange T-shirts, were whispering with two other teammates on the far side of the lawn. One was a small brunette girl with pointed features. The fourth member of Team Fennekin was impossible to miss. He was meaty and tall, towering over all the other kids.

When Stella caught Marco staring, she glared at him. He looked away quickly.

Just then, Logan started chuckling. "Look," he said, pointing. "It really is Professor Birch."

The head counselor stood in the center of the crowd, flipping through papers on his clipboard. All of the camp counselors were named after

Pokémon characters. But Professor Birch was the only one who actually looked the part.

His brown hair was messy, and he had shaved his beard into a goatee that framed his chin. He wore khaki shorts and outdoorsy sandals. And, like the true Professor Birch, he was kind of chubby. It was like he'd stepped straight out of the video game and into Camp Pikachu.

When Professor Birch blew his whistle again, all the campers stood to attention. Then a counselor they called Officer Jenny stepped out of the crowd to explain the rules. She didn't have bluish-green hair like one of the real Officer Jennies. But she wore a blue vest over a white T-shirt. And with her police officer cap, she looked pretty strict.

"It's time for battle, Trainers!" she said. "Are you ready for capture the flag?"

Some of the kids cheered. Others shifted their feet nervously.

"In a few minutes, you'll head back to your secret bases," said Officer Jenny. "You'll hang your flags outside, and then wait for Professor Birch's whistle. That will signal the start of the game. Two of you will head out into the field to try to capture flags. The other two team members will stay back at the secret base to protect your own flag."

Marco and Logan glanced quickly at each other.

We never figured out who would stay and who would go, thought Marco. He was pretty sure Logan would want to capture flags. *But what do I want to do?*

He pictured himself sneaking through the bushes about to grab the Team Fennekin flag. As he reached for the flame-colored cloth, he felt himself suddenly surrounded. Stella towered over him, her eyes narrowed to slits. Sam blocked Marco from behind—seeking revenge for the walnut incident. They raised their arms at the same time, and then, *Splat! Splat! Splat! Splat!*

Marco imagined water balloons pelting him from all directions. Then he saw himself running back to his secret base like a dog with his tail between his legs. Soaking wet. Empty-handed. A big wet loser.

I should probably stay behind, he thought sadly. *I'm just going to let everyone down.*

But after the counselors explained the rules, Nisha had an idea. "We should play Rock, Fire, Grass," she said. "That's the only fair way to decide who stays at the base and who captures flags."

Logan agreed. "Marco and I will go first," he said. He planted his right fist on his left palm. "Let's go, buddy."

Marco reluctantly held out his own hands. Rock, Fire, Grass was like Rock, Paper, Scissors.

Team Treecko had made up the game yesterday using Pokémon types. "Rock" was already a type of Pokémon, but "Paper" and "Scissors" weren't, so they'd plugged in "Fire" and "Grass" instead.

Marco tapped his fist against his hand as he and Logan counted, "One, two . . ." On "three," he flattened his right hand on top of his left. That was the sign for Grass.

Logan kept his hand in a fist, the sign for Rock. When he saw Marco's hands, he sighed. "Grass covers Rock. You win. You get to capture flags." His face fell.

Marco didn't feel like much of a winner. But how could he tell Logan that he would rather stay behind at the secret base?

"I don't get it," said Maddy. "Why does Grass win again?"

"The Grass-type Pokémon are strong against Rock-type," Nisha patiently explained. "Just remember this: Grass grows on Rocks. Rocks put out Fire. And Fire burns Grass. Easy peasy."

Maddy still looked confused, but she put out her hands to play against Nisha. On the count of three, Maddy made the sign for Grass—she flattened her hand. And Nisha made the sign for Fire—she pointed two fingers straight up like flames.

"Fire burns Grass. I win. That means Marco and I get to wear the Balloon Vests!" Nisha said happily.

Marco had almost forgotten about Nisha's invention. But Logan hadn't. When he heard he wouldn't wear the camouflage vest today, he looked more disappointed than ever.

"Race you to the base?" asked Marco, trying to cheer him up.

Logan grinned and took off like a shot.

"Hey, no fair!" said Marco, trailing behind. *But we might as well get this game over with,* he thought. He rounded a bend in the trail and turned on a burst of speed.

"Ooh, it's cold," said Marco, squirming. Nisha was helping him put on the Balloon Vest. It felt squishy and super heavy.

"How's this?" he heard Logan call from outside the tree house. Logan was in charge of sliding the Team Treecko flag into the bracket beside the ladder.

Nisha glanced out the window. "I wish it could be up on the deck," she said. "How can you defend the flag when it's partway down the ladder?"

Marco knew that the counselors had decided where the brackets should go, but the flag did seem pretty low. *Maybe it's so no one will fall trying to capture it,* he thought.

"Don't worry," said Logan confidently. "Maddy and I won't let anyone get the flag."

"That's right," piped up Maddy. "Logan and I make a great team."

Logan turned toward Marco and made a goofy scared face. "Don't leave me here with her!" he whispered. He put his hands together like he was praying. "Take me with you, please! Please!"

Marco laughed, which made him feel less nervous. But when he heard the whistle blow, his stomach lurched.

Time to go, he told himself. *Ready or not.*

CHAPTER FOUR

"There's one!" whispered Nisha, ducking down behind a bush.

Marco glanced over her shoulder and saw it—the chestnut-brown Team Chespin flag. Their secret base was hidden in a grove of pine trees.

"Let's go!" said Nisha, preparing to run for the flag.

"Wait!" whispered Marco, grabbing the back of her orange vest. "Where are they?"

"Who?" asked Nisha.

"Team Chespin!" he said. "If they start beaming us with water balloons, it's going to be hard to get that flag."

Nisha smiled and pointed to his vest. "That's why you have that," she said. "I'll run for the flag, and you cover me. If they start throwing balloons, throw them right back."

Before Marco could argue, she jumped up and sprinted toward the flag. From out of nowhere, two kids in brown T-shirts popped up and bombed her with balloons.

"Cover me!" called Nisha as the first balloon bounced off her shoulder.

Marco stuck his hand into his vest to grab a balloon. But it was stuck! *C'mon!* he thought, tugging harder.

Splat! The balloon burst in his hand, and cold water soaked through his T-shirt.

When Nisha got back to the bushes, she was soaking wet, too. But she flashed a victorious smile as she held up the brown flag. "We got it!"

No thanks to me, thought Marco sadly.

Nisha didn't seem to notice his disappointment. "Let's go!" she said, running for the trees.

Marco raced after her. His vest felt heavier than ever.

Nisha spotted the next secret base, too. A fiery orange flag peeked out from a pile of rocks.

Uh-oh, thought Marco. *Team Fennekin.*

The base looked more like a bear cave than a fox den. Nisha led Marco in a full circle around it, searching for the best way to attack. Marco, meanwhile, kept his eyes peeled for kids in orange T-shirts—with water bombs.

Crack! He stepped on a branch. Nisha whirled around, eyes wide.

Had Team Fennekin heard him, too? Marco stood still for a moment, watching the rocks for movement. There was nothing.

"You go for the flag this time," whispered Nisha. "I'll cover you."

Marco swallowed hard. He flashed back to his dream, wishing that he had Pikachu on his shoulder. Then he remembered the hot breath of the Mightyena on his heels. He shook his head. *Don't think about the dream,* he scolded himself. *Just forget about it already.*

Nisha poked his vest with her elbow. "Go now!" she urged. "Before they see us!"

So Marco stood up. His knees wobbled as he jogged toward the flag.

The first balloon hit him square in the forehead. Then he saw a flash of red, and two more balloons pelted him in the chest.

Get the flag! he told himself. *Keep running!* But with water streaming into his eyes, he couldn't even see the flag. He didn't see Sam stick his leg out from behind a boulder, either—not until it was too late.

Marco tripped and landed hard, scraping his hands and knees,

"Gotcha!" Sam jeered, jumping out from behind the rock.

Marco looked up and took another water bomb in the face. "Stop it!" he hollered, but he knew Sam wouldn't stop—even though Marco was defenseless and on the ground.

Get up, Marco told himself. *Get up!* He used every ounce of energy he had to crawl to his knees and stumble away from Sam.

Then another member of Team Fennekin stepped into his path—the huge boy who looked more like a full-grown man. As Marco dodged away, he could have sworn he heard the boy growl. *Growl like a Mightyena.*

Marco cut a path between Sam and the growling boy. He hit the woods, and kept running. Nisha was calling his name, but he ran even faster. He just ran.

Marco waited until he heard the whistle blow. *Finally,* he thought. *The game is over.*

He left his hiding place in the bushes and made his way back to the Team Treecko secret base.

"There you are!" said Maddy, dangling her feet over the edge of the deck. "We've been waiting for you."

Nisha came out of the tree house behind her. "Where'd you go?" she asked Marco. "I kept calling for you!"

"I . . . um . . . ran out of water balloons," said Marco, patting his flattened vest. It was sort of true. He didn't tell Nisha why all of his balloons were gone. It had happened when he was running away from that big Team Fennekin kid. Marco had glanced over his shoulder for just a second—and run smack into an oak tree.

He remembered the feeling: a gazillion water balloons exploding on him all at once. That explained why his shorts were drenched. He hoped no one would think he'd peed his pants.

"Did you get any flags?" Nisha asked hopefully.

Marco held up his empty hands and hung his head. *Just like in my dream,* he thought sadly. His nightmare had come true.

"Me, neither," said Nisha. "I mean except for the Team Chespin one we got together."

"We lost our flag, too," Maddy confessed, pointing to the empty bracket on the ladder.

"Only because we ran out of water balloons," said Logan, stepping out onto the deck. He looked as disappointed as Marco felt.

"You ran out of balloons, too?" asked Nisha. "There seems to be a lot of that going around." She shot Marco a look and said, "Anyway, we'd better get going. Professor Birch blew his whistle like ten minutes ago."

Marco nodded sadly. As he stepped away from the ladder so that his friends could come down, he nearly slipped. The ground was wet and littered with broken balloons. *Logan and Maddy must have fought pretty hard before losing the flag,* he thought.

Then, as he glanced back up, a patch of color caught Marco's eye. Something was drawn on the smooth bark of a nearby tree.

"Um, guys," he said. "Come here. You have to see this."

"What?" asked Maddy.

"Just get down here," said Marco, louder this time.

One by one, Team Treecko climbed down the ladder and joined Marco. When Logan got there, he sucked in his breath.

On the side of tree, someone had chalked a picture of Treecko. The green gecko-like Pokémon was wearing a diaper and sucking on a baby bottle.

Above him, colorful letters spelled out the words "Team Tickle-Tickle."

"Who did that?" asked Logan.

"Who do you *think* did it?" said Marco, anger creeping into his voice.

The answer hung in the air like a dark storm cloud.

"But when?" said Logan. "We were here the whole time!"

"Fennekin is like a fox, and foxes are sly," Nisha reminded him. "And pretty good artists, too," she added under her breath.

Marco hated to admit it, but Nisha was right. The drawing really did look like Treecko—except for the diaper. Had Stella drawn it? Or one of the other Team Fennekin members? *It couldn't have been Sam. He was back at the base,* thought Marco. He stared at his scraped hands and felt another wave of anger.

Maddy shot Nisha a fierce look. "I don't think it's very good art," she said. Her cheeks were blotchy. Was she thinking about what Sam had said to her? *Wook at da widdle baby.*

Marco wished he could make her feel better. But they hadn't captured Team Fennekin's flag, and Sam wasn't here to fling a thousand walnuts at. After a moment, he asked, "Maddy, how's your mouse doing?"

That perked her up. "He's okay. I fed him a nut. I'm going to bring him more food and water later."

"Good idea," said Marco. "We'll bring some rags and get rid of that ugly drawing." He pointed at the baby Treecko. "It's just chalk. It'll wash right off."

Maddy sniffled and smiled. She seemed happier as Team Treecko walked back to camp. But Nisha and Logan were quiet and gloomy. Marco wished he knew how to make his friends feel better—and himself.

"That was only the first round of capture the flag," he reminded them. "We'll do better tomorrow. We just have to try harder."

"And play smarter," said Nisha. Her eyes had that faraway look, as if she was working on a new invention.

"And aim better," said Logan, "so we don't waste as many balloons."

Maddy stayed silent, a smile playing at the corners of her mouth. She must have been thinking about Dedenne the mouse.

"That's the spirit," said Marco. "We'll get more flags. Tomorrow." But inside his chest, worry niggled. *I sure hope I don't let them down again.*

CHAPTER FIVE

"Where's the Moo-Moo Milk?" Maddy asked at the counter.

"In the refrigerated section, sweetie," said the cashier, a teenage girl wearing a red apron.

Marco chuckled. "I can't believe they actually have Moo-Moo Milk."

Logan shrugged. "Why not? This is a Poké Mart. I'm hoping they sell Mud Balls and Pitfall Mats, too."

Team Treecko had just finished lunch in the Dining Hall. Now they were hoping to buy some things at the Poké Mart to help them do better in tomorrow's round of capture the flag.

But what? thought Marco, scanning the shelves.

"Do you have any Mud Balls?" Logan asked the cashier.

"Mud Balls?" she repeated, raising her eyebrows.

"Yeah, you know, like the secret base decorations in the video game. They burst if you step on them," Logan explained.

When the cashier shook her head, Logan's face fell. "How about Pitfall Mats, the ones that trap you in a pit if you walk on them?" he asked. But he struck out again.

"I can't believe they don't sell Mud Balls or Pitfall Mats," he muttered to Marco. "What kind of a Poké Mart is this?"

Marco could believe it, but he didn't say so. He tried not to laugh.

Nisha stepped up behind them. "We can make our own Mud Balls, Logan. Just buy a bag of water balloons." Then she headed toward the craft section of the store.

When she picked up a long wooden dowel, Marco said, "Nisha must be making something else—some new gadget."

But Logan wasn't even half-listening. "Ooh, Poké Flutes!" he said, grabbing a yellow flute off the shelf. "These are almost as good as Mud Balls. We can use them to lure the enemy away from our base."

"Good idea," said Marco, nodding. He wished he could think of something to buy, too. Nisha had ideas and so did Logan. What about Maddy?

He spotted her blonde pigtails over by the Lava Cookies. *Figures,* he thought, smiling. While Nisha and Logan were preparing for battle, Maddy was buying sweets. *Is she going to fight Team Fennekin with sugar? Rot out their teeth? Give them killer stomachaches?* He laughed out loud.

He didn't have any big ideas for how to win the next round of capture the flag, but at least Maddy didn't either. And that made him feel better—until he saw Sam's red spiky hair bobbing down the aisle toward Maddy.

"Need a boddle for your Moo-Moo Milk, widdle baby?"

Maddy ignored him, marching past to carry her Lava Cookies to the cash register. Her face was lobster red.

Marco's hands balled into fists. *Focus on the game,* he reminded himself. But the truth was, he wanted to take Sam down almost as much as he wanted to capture flags. He wiggled his fingers, trying to shake off the anger. Then he sighed and turned back toward the Poké Flutes, hoping his own good idea would come.

"Am I doing it right?" asked Logan, squirting mud into a balloon.

"Yup," said Nisha. "Half mud, half water. Team Fennekin will never know what hit them."

They were squatting near a puddle by the door of Logan and Marco's cabin. "Making Mud Balls is actually pretty easy," said Logan, passing his mud-filled balloon to Marco.

"Yeah," said Marco, attaching the balloon to the end of the water faucet. "Good thing you didn't pay money for them!"

"And good thing Maddy helped us figure out a way to get the mud into the balloons," said Nisha.

Maddy was sitting on the step eating a Lava Cookie and drinking Moo-Moo Milk. She nodded as she wiped off her milk mustache. "We use pastry bags to decorate Poké Puffs in Professor Sycamore's lab," she said, pointing to the cone-shaped bag in Nisha's hand.

Nisha had filled the pastry bag with mud. The bottom had a pointed metal tip. When she squeezed the bag, mud came out the tip.

This time Nisha didn't argue with the word *lab*. Instead, she handed the full bag to Logan, then stood up and brushed her hands together.

"Okay," she said, "I'd better get working on my other idea."

She wouldn't tell them what it was, but as she was leaving, she asked, "Hey, Maddy, can I have the cap to your Moo-Moo Milk?"

Maddy picked up the metal cap. "This thing? Sure."

Nisha stared at the cap as if it were made of solid gold. Then she tucked it safely into her pocket. "See you later," she said, hurrying off toward the cabin she shared with Maddy. A curious Maddy trailed after her, still munching on her Lava Cookie.

After Marco tied off a few more balloons, Logan said, "Well, I guess we should try these out." He reached for a Mud Ball and stood up.

Marco ducked and held his arm over his face. "You're not going to throw that at me, are you?" He was still having flashbacks from being attacked by water bombs.

Logan laughed. "No!" he said. "Although . . . we could play a game of catch with it."

Pretty soon, the boys were tossing the Mud Ball back and forth—gently—behind the cabin.

"Here's the pitch!" said Logan, tossing the balloon underhand toward Marco.

"It's a fly ball!" called Marco, backing up to catch the balloon in his hands. He flinched, hoping it wouldn't burst in his face.

"Curveball!" he called next, throwing the Mud Ball to Logan. It didn't exactly curve down, though. It was heading straight for Logan's head.

Somehow, Logan caught the Mud Ball without it popping. He set his jaw and sent the balloon right back. "Fastball!" he announced.

Uh-oh, thought Marco. *This isn't going to be good.* Instead of catching the Mud Ball, he dodged out of its path. The balloon looked like it was going to hit the side of the cabin, but it didn't. It plunked straight into a trashcan.

"Yes!" said Logan, pumping his fist. "Three points!"

Marco was about to argue that they were playing baseball, not basketball. But then something strange happened. The garbage can started to shimmy and shake. Both boys stared.

"No way," said Logan.

Marco knew they were both thinking the same thing. In Pokémon games, a shaking trashcan was a sign. It meant that something was hiding inside the can—usually a Pokémon.

Am I dreaming? Marco wondered. *This can't be real!* His heart pounded in his ears.

Logan tiptoed slowly toward the trashcan, but Marco's feet felt like they were stuck in the dirt. *Be careful!* he wanted to holler to Logan. But his throat felt tight and dry.

When Logan was only a foot away, something exploded out of the can.

A flash of yellow fur.

Logan stumbled backward, squealing.

And a muddy Meowth disappeared around the corner with a yeowl.

"Oh, man!" said Logan, half-laughing, half-crying. "That crummy cat! He just gave me a heart attack!"

Marco started laughing, too, and he couldn't stop. Every time he tried to breathe, a new wave of giggles rolled over him. "You should . . . have seen . . . your face!"

Logan fell backward onto the grass and laughed and laughed.

By the time they had both caught their breath, Logan's face was beet red and Marco had the hiccups. He held the side of his stomach, which kind of hurt.

Logan sighed deeply and said, "I'm pretty sure Meowth was spying on us."

"Oh yeah," said Marco, nodding. "He's reporting back to Team Fennekin at this very second. He's telling them all about our Mud Ball plan."

"Because he can talk human, you know," Logan pointed out. "He does it all the time in the cartoons."

"Definitely," said Marco. And then they started laughing all over again.

CHAPTER SIX

Mud Balls are just as heavy as water balloons. Maybe heavier.

That's what Marco decided as he and Logan lugged them to the secret base in their backpacks. Marco stepped carefully on the trail. If he tripped, he'd fall backward and be trapped like a turtle—a turtle with a very muddy back.

When they reached the ladder to the tree house, he stopped short. "Good thing we brought a few extra balloons," he said, staring down at the ground.

"Why?" asked Logan.

"Because I just found a fresh patch of mud." Marco pointed to the base of the ladder. The ground was still wet from where all the water balloons had exploded that morning. Colorful bits of balloon mixed with rocks and walnuts to make a speckled mud collage. It was actually kind of pretty.

"Yes!" said Logan. "We still have those cone thingies to fill them, too. But, wait . . . how will we add water?"

Marco unzipped his backpack and pushed past the bag full of Mud Balls. "We'll use this!" he said, pulling out a spray bottle. He had packed the bottle and a rag to wash the Treecko picture off the tree. But there was enough water in it to fill a few Mud Balls.

Logan opened his own backpack to get the pastry bag, and the boys used sticks to scoop fresh mud into it. A few rocks dropped in accidentally.

"Oops," said Logan. "Should we pick them out?"

Marco thought about it. "Rocks would make the Mud Balls heavier," he said. "And maybe they'd fly faster, like that fastball you threw back at the cabin."

Logan grinned. "That *was* a fastball," he said.

"But rocks are pretty dangerous, too," said Marco with a sigh. "Someone could get hurt."

"Right," said Logan. He looked sort of disappointed, but he carefully picked the rocks out of the pastry bag.

After the boys had filled a few balloons, they stared at the muddy hole left in the ground. "Should we try to fill it in?" asked Marco. "Someone might step in it."

Logan shrugged. "Maybe *Sam* will fall into it," he said. "Wouldn't it be great if we could trap him there? Oh, man . . . I wish they sold Pitfall Mats at the Poké Mart!"

Marco laughed. Then he had an idea—an idea that Nisha would be proud of. "We could use this!" he said, pulling the rag out of his backpack. He spread it carefully over the hole like a welcome mat.

"Cool!" said Logan. "I'd fall for that." He stepped beside the rag and did a fake fall, spinning in a circle and landing on his back in the grass. "Ugh," he said in a raspy voice. "Team Treecko wins again."

When the boys heard the *snap* of a twig in the woods, they both sprang to attention. *Team Fennekin?* Marco wondered.

Nope. It was Maddy hurrying along the trail with a brown paper lunch bag.

"Whatcha guys doing?" she asked.

Marco stepped quickly in front of the Pitfall Mat. "We made a secret trap," he said. "But you have to be careful so that you don't fall into it."

Maddy watched with wide eyes as Marco lifted a corner of the rag, showing her the hole underneath.

She clamped her hand to her mouth, giggling. "Oh, they'll fall for that, for sure," she said.

At the words *fall for that*, Logan performed another fake fall. Only Maddy thought it was a real one. "Are you hurt?" she asked, running over to his side.

Logan jumped up and away from her even more quickly than he had fallen down. "No," he said, his cheeks pink. "I was just kidding. Nothing to see here, folks. I'm all good." He brushed off his shorts and changed the subject. "Where's Nisha?"

Maddy craned her neck to search the trail. "She's behind me somewhere. She's carrying something really heavy."

Sure enough, when Nisha showed up, she had a brown paper bag, too—but hers was supersized.

"Can you help me get it up to the deck?" she asked.

The boys climbed up the ladder, carefully avoiding the Pitfall Mat. Then they passed the brown bag up the ladder from Nisha to Marco and Marco to Logan. When they were inside the tree house, Nisha slid out her new invention.

"It's a tiny tent!" blurted out Logan.

Nisha had attached wooden dowels together with rubber bands. One dowel stuck up above the rest, and she had glued the cap of Maddy's Moo-Moo Milk upside-down to that dowel.

"Is it a house for Dedenne?" Maddy asked hopefully.

Nisha smiled. "No, silly," she said. "It's a cata-pult—a Mud Ball Launcher." She pointed toward the upside-down milk bottle cap. "This is the ammo basket, where you put the Mud Ball. Then you pull the arm back and let it go." She pulled back the top dowel, and when she released it, it snapped and sprang forward.

Marco's fingers itched to try the catapult, but Logan beat him to it. He reached for a Mud Ball and plopped it into the ammo basket.

"Wait, we have to aim it first," said Nisha. She put the catapult in the doorway of the tree house. Then Logan pulled back the arm as far as it would go and released it. The Mud Ball sailed over the deck, past the flag, and down to the ground below. *Splat!*

"Awe-some!" said Logan, racing out the door to see where the Mud Ball had landed.

Maddy seemed less impressed now that she knew the contraption wasn't meant for Dedenne. She was already in the corner feeding her mouse a piece of apple.

But Marco couldn't take his eyes off the cata-pult. "How'd you come up with that?" he asked.

Nisha shrugged. "I made one once for science class," she said with a grin. "That one launched tomatoes, though."

She made it sound like her invention was no big deal, but Marco knew Nisha had worked hard on it. Her fingernails were chewed raw, and she had another Band-Aid on one of her fingertips.

"Logan and I made more Mud Balls," he said, wanting Nisha to know that he had been working hard, too. Then he remembered the Pitfall Mat. As he led Nisha outside to show her, Logan was scrambling back up the ladder.

"Wow," he said. "That catapult has power! Can you launch Team Rocket into space with that thing?"

Marco chuckled. *Just like the end of most Pokémon cartoons,* he thought, imagining Team Rocket getting blasted into the stars. Then he pictured Sam and Stella blasting off instead with shocked looks on their faces, which was even funnier.

Nisha didn't laugh, though. For a second, it looked like she was actually considering building a bigger catapult. Then she shook her head. "Nope. Just Mud Balls."

"That's okay," said Logan. "We'll still get to pummel Team Fennekin with mud." His eyes danced, like he could hardly wait.

Marco couldn't, either. For the first time, he had a good feeling about tomorrow's capture the flag game.

With Mud Balls, a Mud Ball Launcher, and a Pitfall Mat, he wondered, *what could possibly go wrong?*

CHAPTER SEVEN

The next morning, the girls were late—really late.

"Did they forget about the game or something?" asked Marco, staring out the window.

"Probably," said Logan, sounding disgusted. He quickly stepped into his shoes. "Let's go find them."

He and Marco locked their cabin door and ran past the Dining Hall toward the girls' cabins. Nisha was just hurrying out of Cabin Eight.

"Good, they're ready," said Marco, hoping to see Maddy stepping out behind Nisha. But she wasn't there.

"Where's Maddy?" asked Logan.

Nisha sighed. "She was off making Poké Puffs this morning. I thought she'd be back by now."

"Poké Puffs?" said Logan. "At a time like this?"

Marco agreed. "Who has time for Poké Puffs when the next round of capture the flag is about to start?" For the first time, he felt annoyed with Maddy. She sure didn't help out much in planning for the games. And today, she wasn't even here to *play* the game.

Great, he thought. *The day is off to a terrible start.*

They headed to their secret base without Maddy. They didn't have a choice—Professor Birch had already blown the whistle.

When they got to the tree house, Logan hung the flag on the ladder while Nisha set up the Mud Ball Launcher.

"Rock, Fire, Grass?" asked Logan, patting his fist into his palm. "We have to figure out who's staying to defend the base and who's going to grab flags."

Nisha shook her head. "Marco and I went last time, so you and Maddy can go out this time—if she shows up, I mean."

Marco was surprised to see disappointment creep across Logan's face. Didn't he want to capture flags? Then Marco saw him eyeing the catapult.

Nisha saw it, too.

"You'll get your chance with the Mud Ball Launcher," she reminded Logan. "There are three rounds of capture the flag, remember? Besides, you get to wear the Balloon Vest now."

"Ooh!" said Logan, rubbing his hands together. He raced into the tree house to find the camouflage vest.

Marco was relieved to be staying back in the tree house this time, but he still felt nervous. "Maybe I should practice with that," he said, pointing toward the catapult.

"Sure," said Nisha. "Just don't waste too many Mud Balls." She stepped back and let Marco load the Mud Ball Launcher. He pointed it straight out the door of the tree house and pulled back the launching arm.

Snap! The Mud Ball sailed out the door. If someone had been on the ladder reaching for the flag, it would have sent her scrambling back down.

He waited to hear the *splat*. Instead, he heard a squeal.

"Hey!" shouted Maddy from the ground below.

"Oops!" Marco got to his feet and ran out onto the deck. "Are you okay?" he called down.

Maddy looked clean and dry. She must have sidestepped the Mud Ball. But she was hopping mad.

"Look what you made me do!" she said, pointing to a squashed Poké Puff on the ground. "I worked hard on that one, too. It was a Mud Ball Poké Puff for Logan." She held a bakery box in her hands.

Logan popped his head out of the tree house. "You made me a Poké Puff out of mud?" he asked. He actually looked kind of excited by the idea.

"No!" said Maddy. "It wasn't made out of mud. It was chocolate. But *now* it's all muddy." She squatted down and tried to pull the cupcake wrapper out of the chocolaty, muddy mess.

"Sorry," muttered Marco. But he was kind of crabby, too. If Maddy had been here when she was supposed to be, she never would have dropped the cupcake.

Thweet! Professor Birch's whistle blew from the woods beyond.

"Get your vest on, Maddy. Hurry!" said Nisha. "I'll take your Poké Puffs."

She reached for the box, but Maddy swung it out of reach. "No," she said. "I'm taking these with me."

Nisha just stared at her. Marco wanted to argue, too. But why bother? He shook his head and ducked back into the tree house. He had a job to do. Today, he was going to make sure that Team Treecko came out on top—no matter what.

Splat! Splat, splat, splat!

Marco spotted another blue T-shirt through the trees. Team Mudkip was hot on the trail of the Team Treecko flag, but Marco wasn't giving it up without a fight.

He dropped another Mud Ball onto the catapult and pulled back the arm. *Snap!* The Mud Ball sailed into the woods, and he heard someone shriek.

But Team Mudkip kept coming. As a girl with a long brown ponytail raced toward the tree house, Nisha grabbed a Mud Ball from the bin and flung it at the girl. It missed.

Marco grabbed two Mud Balls and hurried out to the deck. He threw one and nailed the girl in the shoulder before she could reach the ladder.

"Ew!" she screamed as mud streamed down her T-shirt. "Gross!"

She ran back into the woods, complaining all the way.

That was the last they saw of Team Mudkip.

"I hope Logan and Maddy are doing as well as we are," said Marco proudly, wiping his hands on his shorts.

Nisha snickered. "Well, I guess if they run out of Mud Balls to throw, they can throw Poké Puffs."

"Right," said Marco, shaking his head at the thought of Maddy carrying that big box into the woods. Then he noticed how empty the bin of Mud Balls was getting. He had brought supplies to make more, but was there time?

He hurried down the ladder and found a wet patch. He had just scooped up some mud and was picking out a rock when Nisha hung her head over the deck. "Incoming!" she whispered, pointing toward a flash of orange in the bushes.

Marco raced back up the ladder, hugging the bowl of mud with one arm while climbing with the other.

As soon as he'd ducked into the tree house, Nisha sprayed the woods with Mud Balls. *Snap, splat! Snap, splat! Snap, splat!*

Then it was quiet.

Marco crawled out onto the deck and peered over the edge.

"Yikes!"

A huge round face stared up at him—the big kid from Team Fennekin. He was so tall, he didn't even have to climb the ladder to reach the flag.

Marco felt a rush of fear, remembering how this guy had pelted him with water balloons outside Team Fennekin's secret base. But as the boy took a step forward, something happened. He stepped onto the Pitfall Mat and fell, toppling like a giant redwood tree.

Timber! Marco wanted to yell, but he didn't. Because the boy was back up in a second trying to get his foot out of the muddy hole.

"I'm stuck!" the boy cried to whoever was still in the woods.

"Quick," Marco called over his shoulder to Nisha. "Throw me a Mud Ball!"

She did, and Marco turned to fling it at the boy below. But the boy was gone! He was limping toward the woods with one shoe on and one very muddy shoe off.

"Yes!" Marco cheered. "Score one for the Pitfall Mat!"

He fought the urge to climb down the ladder and set up the mat again. Maybe this trap could only be used once like the Pitfall Mats in the Pokémon videogames. Besides, there was still another Team Fennekin member in the woods.

Marco scanned the bushes and trees. Was Sam out there? Stella? Someone else? He wasn't sure, but he wasn't going to let anyone sneak by him.

"Check the window," he called to Nisha. She was already there, searching the woods behind the tree house.

Marco took a second to dart back to the Mud Ball Launcher. If Sam or Stella made it to the tree house, they were in for a muddy treat.

But there was only one Mud Ball left!

I'd better make it count, thought Marco, dropping it into the ammo basket.

When a freckled face suddenly appeared above the edge of the deck, Marco yelped with surprise.

"Ha! Caught you napping, you big baby," said Sam, reaching for the flag.

Marco felt a wild rush of anger. No way was he letting Team Fennekin get the flag—especially not smart-mouthed Sam. No way.

He pulled back the arm of the catapult so far he feared it would break. Then he let it go. *Snap!*

The Mud Ball flew toward Sam's head and then . . . sailed right over his shoulder.

Sam ducked as he slid the flagpole out of its bracket. "Missed me, ya big loser," he said, snickering.

Marco searched frantically around the catapult, hoping to find another Mud Ball. There weren't any. *Now what?* Eyeing the bowl of fresh mud, he scooped up a huge handful and pressed it into the Mud Ball Launcher.

This time, he wouldn't miss. This time, Sam was going down.

Marco launched a fastball off the catapult. It hit Sam smack in the forehead and wiped the smirk right off his face. He hung there for a moment in mid-air, and then he dropped.

When Sam hit the ground, there was silence.

Uh-oh. Marco felt a chill run down his spine. Something was wrong.

He crawled to the edge of the deck and saw Sam lying on the ground below, his eyes wide. It looked like he couldn't breathe—like the wind had been knocked right out of him.

And there was something else.

A thin trail of blood trickled off Sam's forehead and onto the ground below.

CHAPTER EIGHT

"I'm sorry," Marco said again. "It was an accident—honest."

Sam wouldn't even look at him. He was leaning back against a tree, tears and snot running down his face. But at least his forehead had stopped bleeding.

Marco checked the trail, hoping to see Nisha. She had sprinted off to get help, and then he'd heard the sound of a whistle. That meant she had found someone. A counselor should be showing up any minute now.

Not soon enough, thought Marco, picking at the grass nervously. He'd probably get in trouble, but at least there'd be someone here to help Sam.

Sam didn't look like a bully anymore. In fact, he looked like a little kid leaning against that tree. Above him, the drawing of Treecko in diapers was still fresh. Marco had forgotten to wash it off. Now the gecko-like Pokémon looked down on Sam as if to say, "Who's da widdle baby now?"

Marco wanted to laugh, but he couldn't. Not when Sam was hurt and crying—all because of something he'd done.

Finally, *finally* Nisha came running back with Officer Jenny behind her. Marco gulped. He had been hoping for Professor Birch, who wasn't as strict. *Is she going to arrest me?* he wondered, staring up at Officer Jenny's pinched face.

She squatted beside Sam and lifted his hand off his forehead. "Let me see," she said, inspecting his cut.

Sam winced as she pressed on his skin and felt for a bump.

"Does anything else hurt?" she asked him.

As Sam shook his head no, Marco heard more people pushing through the brush. Maddy appeared, still carrying her box of Poké Puffs. And Logan jogged up behind her, waving two flags: the aqua Team Froakie flag and the sunshine-yellow Team Torchic flag.

"Victory!" he called, until he saw Sam. "Oh."

"What happened?" asked Maddy, her face filled with concern. She dropped to her knees beside Sam, as if he were an injured animal.

"Yes, what did happen exactly?" asked Officer Jenny. Marco half-expected her to pull out a notebook and start doing a real police investigation.

"It was an accident. I, um, hit him with a Mud Ball," Marco confessed.

"A what?" asked Officer Jenny.

"A water balloon," explained Nisha. "With a little mud in it."

"Ah," said Officer Jenny, nodding. Then she glanced back at Sam's cut. "But how did you break the skin with a soft, squishy water balloon?"

Silence hung like a heavy curtain. The Marco said in a quiet little voice, "I ran out of balloons and just used mud, and it's possible . . . I mean maybe . . . the mud had a rock in it."

Officer Jenny raised an eyebrow. Nisha and Maddy looked surprised, too.

"A rock?" asked Maddy. "Ouch, that must have hurt." She patted Sam's leg.

Sam scowled at her until she pointed to her bakery box and asked, "Do you want a Poké Puff?"

He opened his mouth as if he were going to say something nasty. Then he clamped it shut again and shrugged. "Sure, I guess," he said, wiping his nose with his arm.

Maddy chose carefully, giving him a fancy cake with red sprinkles. He took it and actually mumbled *thanks* before biting into the chocolate frosting.

Marco wondered whether Maddy would suddenly look up and see the Treecko on the tree. Would she be furious with Sam all over again? *Or will she be mad at me for not washing it off?* he wondered.

She didn't get angry. Instead, Maddy fussed over Sam as if he were Dedenne, her pet mouse with the bum leg. And, for the first time, Marco was glad that Maddy had been baking like crazy. Her Poké Puffs had saved the day.

Now that Sam was feeling better, Officer Jenny seemed more relaxed, too. When she helped Sam to his feet and toward the trail, Marco breathed a huge sigh of relief. It didn't look like he was going to get in trouble after all.

"How do you know there were rocks in the mud?" asked Nisha as Team Treecko climbed back up to the tree house. Officer Jenny might have let the rock thing go, but Nisha wasn't going to.

"Because I found one," said Marco sadly. He held up his palm to reveal a muddy stone. It was gray, heavy, and sharp.

Maddy sucked in her breath. "Ooh," she said. "That's a rock all right."

When Nisha chuckled, Maddy whirled around to scold her. "What's so funny?" she asked.

Nisha shrugged. "Sorry. I was just thinking about how Fennekin is a Fire-type Pokémon. And you know what type works best against Fire?"

Logan thought of it before Marco could. "Rock!" he shouted.

"Right," said Nisha. "Fire burns Grass, Grass covers Rock, and Rock puts out Fire. Marco took out Team Fennekin with a rock. Isn't that kind of weird?"

Logan laughed, too, but Marco couldn't. "It was an accident," he said again, wiping the mud off the stone with the edge of his T-shirt. Then he stuck the rock in his pocket, hoping everyone would just stop talking about it already.

Nisha straightened up. "I know it was an accident," she said firmly. "And, anyway, Sam is okay."

"And in other news," said Logan cheerily, "I scored two flags!" He held them up and waved them in the air. "Actually, it was really Maddy who won them."

"Wait, what?" said Marco.

Nisha's eyebrows lifted in surprise.

"You should have seen it," said Logan. "She distracted Team Froakie with Poké Puffs. She walked right up to their base and offered them cupcakes, and then I snuck over and grabbed the flag. It worked with Team Torchic, too. They didn't even know what happened!"

He leaned over to give Maddy a high-five.

"See?" she said, beaming. "I told you we made a great team."

This time Logan didn't argue.

Marco should have felt happy. Instead, he felt guilty. Just a few hours ago, he'd been angry at Maddy because he thought she was baking instead of helping her team. But she *had* been helping her team—fighting the enemy with sweet surprises just like a Fairy-type Pokémon would.

I guess Maddy did *have a plan,* he thought sadly. *Everyone's had a plan that worked, except for me.*

"Hey, did you have fun with the Mud Ball Launcher?" asked Logan, tapping the ammo basket so that it bobbed up and down.

"Yes!" said Nisha. "Marco and I made a pretty good team, too. We fought off two attacks and protected the flag."

Marco was about to agree, but then he remembered something. Just before he'd hit Sam with the glob of mud, Sam had stolen the flag. Where was it now?

Marco hurried out to the deck and searched the ground. There it was—the lime-green flag was wadded up in a ball in the muddy grass below. He sank back onto his knees.

"We didn't protect the flag," he said softly.

"What?" asked Nisha.

"Sam took it out of the holder before I could stop him," said Marco, more loudly this time. He wasn't happy about it, but he had to be honest. "Sam won it fair and square."

So as Team Treecko trudged back to camp, Logan carried the Team Froakie and Team Torchic flags high. And Marco carried the Team Treecko flag—a little lower. But somehow, bringing the flag to Sam made Marco feel better.

Sam might call me a loser, but at least he can't call me a liar. He tightened his grip on the flag and marched on.

CHAPTER NINE

"Shh!" said Nisha. "They're interrupting the movie to bring us the Great Flag Hunter update." She pointed to the big screen on the other side of the Media Center.

"I can't look," groaned Logan, covering his face with his hands.

But Marco took in the screen. There it was, in black and white:

Team Fennekin: 2 points (2 flags captured, 0 flags lost)
Team Treecko: 1 point (3 flags captured, 2 flags lost)

The other teams trailed with zero or even negative points. But Marco couldn't see past his own team's score. If he hadn't given Sam the flag this morning, Team Treecko would be in the lead. *Are my teammates mad at me?* he wondered.

Logan wouldn't take his hands off his face—even when Maddy offered him half of her Lava Cookie. "Not now," he mumbled. "I lost my appetite." But he peeked at her through his fingers.

A *whoop* came from the corner of the room, which meant Team Fennekin had seen the scores, too. Sam and Stella were playing the Pokémon trading card game at a small wooden table. Even from Marco's spot on the couch, he could see the nasty bruise on Sam's forehead. It made him look sort of tough. But Marco knew better. He could still picture Sam sitting under that tree with tears streaming down his face.

Marco tried to focus on the Pokémon movie that had started again on the screen. When Logan hopped up to act out some of Pikachu's fight moves, Marco craned his neck to see. "Logan, sit down!" he said, scooting over on the couch.

But now he was distracted by Maddy, who was playing something weird on the handheld video game she had checked out from the Media Center. She raised the game in front of her face and smiled at the screen. She blinked, opened her mouth wide, and tilted her head back and forth. Marco burst out laughing—she looked so funny!

"What?" she said, glancing up innocently.

"What are you doing?" he asked.

"It's the Making Faces game!" she said. "Whatever I do, my Pokémon does. And sometimes it tells me what to do, too. Oh, here—he wants me to make a kissy face."

When Maddy started kissing her game, Logan shot Marco a disgusted look. He grabbed his throat and pretended to be throwing up behind her, until Maddy spun around and caught him.

"Hey! Mind your own business," she said. "I'm bonding with my Pokémon."

"You should try it, too," Nisha said to Logan. "It helps your Pokémon evolve."

"No, thanks," said Logan. "No kissing for me. I'd rather lose. I'd rather *die.*"

He faked a dramatic death right there on the rug of the Media Center. Everyone pretty much ignored him except for Nisha, who rolled her eyes.

Marco might have laughed, but Nisha's words about evolution had just reminded him of something. He picked up his own videogame, which he had paused for the movie.

"Okay, Charizard," he said. "Time to battle Fletchling." Charizard was an orange, dragon-like Pokémon. And Marco finally had the Mega Stone he needed to help him Mega Evolve.

Marco selected a move and then it happened— in a flash of light, Charizard transformed. The orange dragon turned into a fierce gray-black dragon. Blue flames leaped from his mouth.

"He did it!" Marco blurted out. "Charizard Mega Evolved!"

"Cool," said Nisha. "Did his type change?"

"What?" said Logan, looking away from the movie screen. "Pokémon can't change types."

"They can if they Mega Evolve," said Nisha. "But it's only a temporary change."

Marco was about to check the stats on his game when he heard an outburst from across the room.

"Knock-out!" Stella cried, jumping up from the table. "And that was a Pokémon-EX card, so I win two prize cards for that. I win. You lose, Sammy Whammy. Oh, well. Too bad for you."

Sam rubbed his forehead as if his injury had made him play badly. "Wait," he said. "Look! My card has a resistance to your card, so I subtract twenty from the damage. Now it's not a knock-out." He slid two discs off the card.

Stella put her hand on her hip and stared. "Let me see that," she said, reaching for the card with her other hand.

Sam gave it to her, but instead of looking at it, she immediately slid it into her back pocket. "Thanks for the gift," she said. "It's all mine now. See ya later, loser."

She turned away with a smirk on her face and pranced out the door.

"Wow, what a bully," said Logan, watching Stella go.

But Marco couldn't take his eyes off Sam's face. It looked red and blotchy, kind of like Maddy's right before she cried. Was he going to cry again?

As Sam got up to leave, Marco blurted out, "Sam, wait a sec. I have to ask you something." He hadn't even thought it through. The words had just sprung from his lips.

Sam stared suspiciously at Marco, as if he were ready to duck another Mud Ball—or to throw one.

Marco racked his brain trying to figure out what to say. Finally, he asked in his friendliest voice, "So, what card did Stella take?"

Sam muttered something under his breath.

"What was that?" asked Marco.

"It was my Magnezone-EX," said Sam.

"Oh, wow," said Nisha.

"Full-art version," Sam continued. "Ultra rare."

Even Logan was paying attention now. "That's a good card."

"And it was holofoil," Sam added sadly.

"Huh?" asked Maddy.

"That means it was shiny," whispered Nisha.

Marco whistled under his breath. Now he knew why Sam was so upset. Maddy seemed to sense it, too. She crossed the room until she was standing right in front of Sam. Then she smiled and tilted her head—first to one side and then to the other.

Is she trying to bond with him like she did with her Pokémon? Marco wondered. *Is she going to give him her kissy face next?* He snickered a little.

Sam couldn't figure out Maddy's game either. "What are you doing?" he asked, leaning back.

She blinked at him slowly, still smiling.

When Sam looked like he was about to say something mean, Maddy pulled a cookie out of the front pouch of her sweatshirt. "Want my Lava Cookie?" she asked quickly.

"Hey, I thought that was for me!" Logan piped up.

Maddy glanced at Logan and shrugged. "You snooze, you lose, mister," she said before turning back to Sam with her best smile.

Sam reached for the cookie. "Thanks," he said, taking a bite and spraying crumbs onto the floor.

As he walked away, he seemed to have forgotten all about his full-art, ultra-rare Magnezone-EX trading card with holofoil.

"What was that all about?" Nisha asked Maddy.

"I think she was bonding with him," explained Marco.

Maddy grinned and nodded. "I was trying to help him Mega Evolve."

Logan snorted. "He's not a Pokémon, Maddy. Bullies can't change their type."

Maddy turned to face him. "You're just mad because he ate your cookie," she said, putting her hands on her hips.

As the two of them squabbled about Lava Cookies and Mega Evolution, Marco watched Sam leave the Media Center. *Can a bully change?* Marco wondered. *And is Sam even a bully?* A few minutes ago, it looked like Stella was the one bullying him.

"Well, even if Sam could evolve, he'd need a Mega Stone," said Nisha. "Charizard needs the Charizardite Mega Stone. Sam would need a Samuelite Mega Stone. And I'm pretty sure we aren't going to find any Samuelites here at Camp Pikachu." She giggled, cracking up over her own joke.

Maddy was confused. "We might be able to find a Samuelite," she said. "We could at least look!"

Logan shook his head in disbelief. "Maddy, she was kidding. There's no such thing as a Samuelite Mega Stone."

As Maddy stuck out her tongue at Logan, Marco put his hand in his pocket. The stone was still there with bits of dry mud clinging to it. He almost pulled it out and made his own joke. But the memory of Sam's bleeding forehead was too fresh. Marco shook his head and stuffed the "Samuelite" back down.

CHAPTER TEN

Marco crouched low in the grass with Pikachu at his side. Would they hear the noise again? He held his breath and strained his ears.

There it was! The faint yipping sound came from Marco's left—no, from straight ahead. It seemed to bounce off the bushes and trees surrounding the grassy field.

"Pi-ka-chuuuu," said his Pokémon friend in a quiet, cautious voice.

But when Marco turned to reassure him, it wasn't Pikachu squatting in the grass. It wasn't a friend at all.

It was a Mightyena.

Marco couldn't look away from its red, glowing eyes. As a deep growl rose from the fierce Pokémon's throat, Marco froze.

He couldn't run. He couldn't fight. There wasn't time.

Instead, he dared to make the tiniest move. He tilted his face to the right.

The Mightyena stopped growling just for a moment. Slowly, he cocked his head to the right to mirror Marco's.

Then Marco slowly—very slowly—cocked his head to the left.

When the Mightyena did the same thing, Marco smiled.

But instead of smiling back at him, the Mightyena bared his teeth and growled. He snapped at the air just in front of Marco's nose.

Marco tried to stay perfectly still, a bead of sweat trickling down the side of his face. His nose suddenly itched—badly—but he couldn't scratch it. If he raised his arm, the Mightyena would attack!

Now the itch felt stronger than ever. He couldn't stand it any more. As he raised his hand oh-so-slowly to scratch his nose, the Mightyena growled, flattened his back, and sprang forward. . . .

"Ay-yah!" screamed Marco, bolting upright. His videogame dropped to the rug.

He was lying on the couch in the Media Center, where he must have dozed off. And someone was laughing hysterically beside him.

Logan.

"Gotcha!" said Logan, reaching out to tickle Marco's nose again with his fingertip.

Marco swatted at Logan's hand. "Not funny!" he told his friend. "I thought you were a Mightyena about to eat my face off." He took a deep breath and rubbed his eyes.

Suddenly, Maddy raced into the room. She looked like she had just come face-to-face with a Mightyena, herself. "He's gone!" she cried, fat tears rolling down her cheeks.

"Who?" Marco and Logan asked at the same time.

"Ded . . . enne!" Maddy stammered. "Someone took him!"

"Maybe he just chewed his way out of the box," said Nisha as they hurried through the woods.

"No!" said Maddy angrily. "I told you—the whole box is gone. Somebody took my mouse."

When she started sprinting again, Marco grabbed his waist and tried to squeeze out his side ache. Maddy could actually run pretty fast when she was upset.

"Did you . . . bring him to your cabin . . . and just forget you did?" asked Logan, who was nearly out of breath, too.

Maddy gave him the stink-eye over her shoulder and kept running.

Sure enough, when they reached the tree house, Dedenne and his shoebox were gone. Maddy collapsed in a heap on the floor and started to whimper.

"Who's going to f-feed him?" she said, her voice quivering. "Who will t-take care of him?"

"I think the real question is who took him," said Marco. He locked eyes with Logan and Nisha. "Team Fennekin?"

Logan nodded slowly. "Who else?" he asked.

"But Sam and Stella were at the Media Center with us today," said Marco. "When would they have come here?"

Nisha chewed her fingernail. "They left before we did. And there was lots of time before lunch, too."

"Wait, what's this?" asked Maddy in a tiny voice. She picked something up from the floor, held it between her fingertips, and stared at it.

Nisha bent over to see. "It looks like a chocolate crumb," she said. "Is that from one of your chocolate Poké Puffs?"

Maddy shrugged. Then she did something unexpected. She popped the crumb into her mouth and ate it.

"Gross!" said Nisha. "That floor is dirty."

Maddy ignored her. But after she swallowed the crumb, her face darkened. "Lava Cookie," she said in a low voice. "Definitely a Lava Cookie."

"So it was Sam!" said Logan, his eyes blazing. "Sam took Dedenne."

"Even after Maddy shared her cookie with him." Nisha shook her head. "I guess bullies don't change after all."

Marco felt anger and something else—disappointment—swell in his chest. *Sam is a bully after all. I guess I was wrong about him.*

When Logan announced that they should track down Sam right away and get the mouse back, Marco was all in.

"I'm going, too," said Maddy. "Dedenne needs me. He won't be scared if he sees me."

"Count me in," Nisha added.

"Should we do Rock, Fire, Grass to see who goes?" asked Logan.

Marco shook his head. "We don't need to. This time, we should all stick together." He threw out his hand in the center of their circle, palm down. His friends quickly piled their hands on top.

"Team Treecko," he said firmly.

"Team Treecko," Logan and Nisha echoed.

"Team Treecko," added Maddy. She wiped her face and smiled.

"Does it look like anyone is there?" Marco whispered through the brush. He had led his team to the rocky Team Fennekin fortress.

Logan was standing on his tiptoes peeking through the window—a small hole in the rocks. He lowered himself to the ground and shook his head. "It's empty. C'mon." Marco followed Logan around the rocks toward the narrow entrance. He heard Nisha and Maddy stepping out of the bushes behind him.

The inside of the cave was dark and chilly. As Marco's eyes adjusted, he could see a few shapes: A bucket of water balloons filled for tomorrow's game. The orange Team Fennekin flag, rolled and ready to hang out front. Was there a shoebox, too? He couldn't tell.

"Nice," said Nisha, stepping inside. "This is almost as cool as our tree house."

"Is he in here?" asked Maddy. The only thing on her mind was finding her mouse.

"I don't see him," said Marco.

Maddy started searching every nook and cranny.

Logan, meanwhile, was looking out the window—the same window he had just been peering into from the other side. "Get down!" he whispered suddenly. "Someone's coming!"

Uh-oh, thought Marco. The first person he pictured was the giant Team Fennekin kid, the one who had pelted him with water bombs. Just being back at this secret base gave Marco the willies.

Logan didn't waste a second, though. As footsteps crunched in the gravel out front, he reached for a water bomb. *Splat!* The shadowy figure in the doorway went down.

"Hey!" someone hollered.

Sam! thought Marco, instantly recognizing the voice. Were the other Team Fennekin kids behind him?

Sam sat up and wiped his face.

"Are you alone?" Logan asked sharply.

"Yes! I mean, no," said Sam, his eyes wild. "My team is going to be here any minute. You guys better get out of there, or else—"

Is he lying? Marco wondered. He sure looked scared.

"Where's my mouse?" Maddy demanded. She got right in Sam's face, her hands on her hips.

"Your what?" asked Sam, ducking as if she were about to hit him.

"You know what I'm talking about," said Maddy, sounding fierce. "Give him back."

"I don't know anything about your dumb mouse!" said Sam. But he wouldn't look at her. He seemed suddenly afraid of the seven-and-a-half-year-old girl.

"You were there. We know you were!" said Logan. "You went to our tree house. We saw the cookie crumbs inside."

Sam's face went pale. Then he started talking really fast. "I was . . . I mean, I did go to your tree house. But I only climbed up and looked around—for, like, a second. I didn't take anything. Honest, I didn't!"

"Right," said Logan. "Keep talking, liar."

Marco tried to keep his voice steady. "So, why did you go there, then? Why did you go to our secret base?"

Sam bit his lip as if he were trying to keep his mouth shut.

"See?" said Logan. "You're nothing but a liar. Liar, liar, pants on fire."

"I was trying to do something nice," Sam finally blurted out. "But I guess that was a big mistake."

Logan snorted. "Nice? Yeah, right."

Nisha narrowed her eyes like she didn't believe Sam either.

But Marco wasn't so sure. Something about Sam's expression said that he was telling the truth.

Maddy must have thought so, too. As Sam stared glumly down at the ground, she cocked her head. She studied his face, as if she were playing the Making Faces game all over again. Then she uncrossed her arms and slumped back against the rock wall.

"Sam didn't take my mouse," she announced.

"How do you know?" asked Logan. "Prove it, Sam. What was this 'nice' thing you did?"

Sam groaned and pulled a wet, soggy paper towel out of his pocket. "I just went to clean something up," he said. The paper towel was covered in colorful chalk.

Maddy stared at the towel, her forehead wrinkled in confusion. Logan snorted again. But Marco knew exactly what Sam had just done.

"You cleaned the Team Treecko picture off the tree?" he asked.

Sam nodded slowly.

"Really?" said Nisha.

Sam shrugged. "Well, I tried to wash it off. Mostly it just smeared the colors around."

Logan wasn't backing down. "Why'd you draw that picture in the first place?" he asked.

"I didn't!" said Sam firmly.

And, again, Marco believed him. He had seen Sam at Team Fennekin's secret base yesterday. He couldn't have been the artist.

"Did Stella do it?" Marco asked.

Sam stayed quiet as if he didn't want to rat out his sister. But he didn't deny it, either.

"Did Stella take my mouse, too?" Maddy asked, towering over Sam again.

"I don't know!" he said. "I told you—I never saw your mouse. But if she took it, she probably brought it back to her cabin. That's what she did with my Magnezone-EX Pokémon card."

Everyone fell silent. Getting a mouse out of Stella's locked cabin would be hard—just as hard as capturing the flag from Team Fennekin's secret base. Maybe even harder.

"We need a plan," said Marco. Instantly, all eyes turned toward him—even Sam's.

CHAPTER ELEVEN

"We should knock on Stella's door and then bomb her and that other Team Fennekin girl with Mud Balls," Logan suggested.

Sam shot Logan a hurt look. Marco could still see the bruise on Sam's forehead even in the dark of the cave.

"No more Mud Balls," said Marco firmly. *No walnuts. No more people getting hurt.* "This time we should fight fire with . . ."

"Fire?" asked Nisha, trying to guess.

"No," said Marco. "We'll fight Fire with . . . Fairy." He smiled at Maddy. "I think we're going to need more Poké Puffs."

Maddy's eyes brightened.

"Yeah!" said Logan. "You could lure Stella and that other girl away from their cabin just like you did during capture the flag. And then the rest of us can go inside and rescue Dedenne."

Maddy smiled wide.

"But wait, how will we know when Stella will be in her cabin?" asked Nisha.

"I could tell you," said Sam in a small voice.

"No, thanks," said Logan harshly. "We don't need your help."

"Well, we *might* need his help," Marco argued.

Sam nodded. "I could give you a signal or something," he said. "Like after dinner."

"That would give us time to prepare," said Nisha.

"And bake," said Maddy.

But Logan pushed back. "I don't trust Sam," he said, as if Sam weren't sitting there beside him. "I think he's going to tell Team Fennekin all about our plan. Why wouldn't he?"

"Because," said Marco. The answer had just come to him. "Sam is going to help us. If he does, we might be able to help him get his Magnezone-EX Pokémon card back."

"Really?" said Sam, sitting up straight.

Marco shrugged. "Maybe," he said. "We can try. If it's in Stella's room, we might be able to find it."

Sam looked pretty happy about that.

Logan didn't look thrilled with the plan, but he stopped arguing. "Fine," he said, crossing his arms at his chest. "Sam can help."

Sam's knock came much later than Marco had expected. He and Logan were sitting in their cabin at dusk when Sam poked his head in. Nisha and Maddy were right behind him.

"She's there," said Sam. "Stella's in her cabin. You should go right now!"

"Finally!" said Logan, pushing away from the wall. "It's almost dark out."

"That's why I packed the Head Lights," said Nisha proudly.

"The head lice?" said Sam, wrinkling his nose.

"No!" said Nisha in disgust. "I said Head *Lights*." She reached into her navy blue shoulder bag and pulled out her latest invention: baseball caps with tiny flashlights strapped to the brims. She put one on her head and handed two more to Logan and Marco.

Marco put his on and flipped the switch a couple of times, which made light dance across the cabin wall.

Logan slapped his hands over his eyes.

"Stop—it's too bright!" wailed Logan. "I'm blind! I'm blind!" He peeked at Marco from between his fingers and started laughing.

"You're in a good mood all of a sudden," said Marco. He was glad that Logan wasn't crabby anymore about including Sam.

"That's because I'm about to go off on a secret mission," said Logan. He reached for the camouflage Balloon Vest hanging on the back of his desk chair.

"Are there Mud Balls in there?" asked Maddy.

Logan shook his head. "Just my Poké Flute." He slid his hand into the vest and pulled out the yellow flute he'd bought at the Poké Mart yesterday.

"What are you going to do with that?" asked Maddy.

Logan smiled mysteriously. "You'll see."

Maddy sighed impatiently. But she was carrying her own weapon: a box of freshly baked Poké Puffs.

The smell of the cupcakes drifted through the taped seams of the box, which made Marco drool. *Don't think about them,* he told himself. *There's no time for snacking. We have a job to do.*

"C'mon!" Sam said again from the doorway. "I'll show you which cabin is Stella's."

As Maddy turned to follow him, she adjusted the water bottle strapped to her back.

"Why do you need water?" asked Logan.

"You'll see," Maddy said in a sly voice.

Marco chuckled. Logan wouldn't tell Maddy his secret, and now she wasn't going to tell him hers, either. But Logan didn't think it was so funny. He punched Marco in the arm.

"Ouch!" said Marco, still laughing.

Then it was time to go. As all five kids tiptoed into the dark, Logan flicked on his Head Light.

"Not yet!" Marco whispered, gesturing toward the counselors' cabin.

Logan fumbled with his hat, trying to turn off the flashlight. It fell to the ground, casting a tunnel of light toward the stars above.

Marco froze, listening for sounds in the cabin. Was Professor Birch in there watching them from a dark window? He counted to ten before finally letting out his breath and tiptoeing forward.

When they reached the Dining Hall, Team Treecko separated.

Maddy set her Poké Puffs on a bench just outside the Dining Hall. Then she sat down beside them and waved good-bye to her teammates.

Logan turned on his Head Light and ran toward the clearing in front of the woods, pulling his flute out of his vest.

Marco and Nisha followed Sam toward Stella's cabin. But while Sam knocked on the door, they hid around the corner and listened.

Stella didn't answer on the first knock.

Uh-oh, thought Marco. *Was Logan right? Did Sam set us up?*

Stella finally opened the door, and Marco heard Sam say, "Hey, do you have any money? Someone is selling fresh Poké Puffs over at the Dining Hall. Let's go check them out. You, too, Claire."

Stella said something snarky—Marco couldn't quite make out the words. But she must have had a sweet tooth like her brother, because she stepped out of the cabin, her purse jingling with change. Marco heard the sound of flip-flops. Was that Claire, the other girl on Team Fennekin?

The door clicked shut. Marco hoped Sam had been the one to close it—and that he had remembered to leave it unlocked.

"Let's go!" Nisha urged, nudging his shoulder.

Marco glanced around the corner to make sure the coast was clear. A soft light burned from the window of the counselors' cabin nearby. *Is Officer Jenny in there?* he wondered. She had eagle eyes. He'd better be quick about this.

Marco took a deep breath and sprinted toward Stella's cabin. The door opened easily. *Phew!*

As he and Nisha stepped through the door-way, a flash of yellow fur streaked past them into the cabin. "Yikes!" said Nisha, jumping backward. "What was that?"

A low yeowl near the dresser gave Marco his answer. "Looks like Meowth is going to help us search," he said.

The cat was on his hind legs scratching at the top drawer of the dresser, which was open just a hair.

"Is he trying to tell us something?" asked Nisha thoughtfully.

Marco cocked his head. "Maybe. Logan says Meowth speaks human. But right now I think he's speaking mouse." He hurried toward the drawer. Sure enough, as he pulled it open, Dedenne's shoe-box slid into view. When Marco lifted the lid, the mouse looked up, his whiskers trembling.

"Wow, that was easy!" said Nisha. "Is he okay?"

Marco nodded. "I think so, but we can't let Meowth get his claws into him." He replaced the lid again firmly just in time. Meowth leaped onto the dresser and sniffed at the box. Maddy had poked air holes into the lid, but they were too small for cat paws to get through.

"Get away from there!" said Marco, trying to shoo the cat off the dresser. He didn't dare touch him. Meowth had sharp claws, a chewed-up ear, and a crooked tail. He had been in his share of fights, and Marco didn't want to be his next victim.

Then he remembered something that his cats at home liked to do. He turned on his Head Light, which sent a ball of light bouncing along the cabin wall.

Meowth spotted it instantly and pounced, trying to capture the light.

Nisha laughed. "Okay, enough already. There's no time to play. Let's get out of here!"

"Wait," said Marco. "We have to find one more thing." He scanned the room in search of Pokémon trading cards.

Nisha put her hand on her hip. "Are we really going to try to find Sam's Pokémon card?" she asked. "It could be anywhere! And we're running out of time."

Marco didn't listen. Sam had helped them out, and now Marco wanted to help him, too. That was the fair thing to do.

He searched the table beside the bed. He didn't know for sure which bed was Stella's, but he figured the one with the magenta blanket was a safe bet. The blanket had skulls and crossbones on it—another sign that it belonged to scary Stella.

Nisha suddenly sucked in her breath. "They're coming!" she said, pointing toward the cracked front door.

Marco quickly turned off his Head Light and stood stock still, barely breathing.

"Don't you hear it?" Sam was saying loudly.

"Hear what?" Stella snapped. She sounded annoyed.

"That music!" said Sam. "It's coming from the woods. We should check it out."

"It sounds like a flute," said another girl—probably Claire. "I wonder who's playing it?"

Stella must have wondered, too, because their voices grew quiet again as they walked away.

Marco let out his breath and smiled into the shadows, hoping Logan was well hidden in those woods. The camouflage vest would help.

Nisha closed the door and sighed with relief. "That was way too close. We need to get out *now*."

"Just a second," said Marco. Logan had bought them some time with the Poké Flute. Would it be enough time to find the Pokémon card?

He turned his Head Light back on and searched the pile of books and papers on Stella's nightstand. A sketch pad was open, which showed a colored-pencil drawing of a fierce Fennekin. It was a really good drawing. Stella was definitely the artist who drew Treecko on that tree.

Then Marco saw the book tossed on Stella's pillow. Something glittered up at him—something tucked between the pages.

He picked up the book and flipped it open. "Magnezone-EX," he said under his breath.

"Full-art, ultra rare version?" asked Nisha.

"With holofoil," Marco added, grinning. He slid the card into his back pocket and dropped the book back onto the bed. "Okay, now we can get out of here. Let's get Dedenne."

"Wait a minute," said Nisha. "I just had an idea."

Marco was going to argue, but Nisha's ideas were usually pretty good ones. He watched her as she inspected Dedenne's shoebox. "Here, take him out of the there," she said, holding the box toward Marco.

"What?"

"Pick up the mouse!" she urged. "Hurry up!"

Before Marco knew it, he was holding the mouse in his hands, its paws and whiskers tickling his fingers. *Pretend it's a pet hamster,* he told himself, trying to stay calm.

Nisha fiddled with the box and then set it back in Stella's dresser drawer. "Now we can go," she said. But as she turned toward the window, she suddenly ducked. "They're standing right outside. With Maddy!"

Marco turned toward the window, too, and when he did, Maddy spotted him. Her eyes grew wide. Then he heard her say in her sweetest voice,

"Do you want to try another Poké Puff, Stella? For free?"

What Maddy didn't see was Officer Jenny walking up right behind her. Marco sucked in his breath. He could barely watch.

"What's going on here?" asked the counselor, stepping into the circle of kids.

"Oh! Um, fresh Poké Puffs," Sam said quickly. "Would you like one?"

Yes, give her one! thought Marco. It would sweeten Officer Jenny right up. But instead of offering her a cupcake, Maddy stood frozen.

Officer Jenny glanced into the box and said, "No, better not. I've had too many Poké Puffs lately." She patted her stomach and winked at Maddy. "Now let's break things up here and get back to your cabins. Lights out soon."

"Yes, ma'am," said Sam.

As the counselor walked away, Marco slowly blew out his breath.

Maddy seemed more relaxed, too, as she held her bakery box toward Stella. "Do you want this one?" she asked, pointing toward a cake. "It's my newest flavor. No one has ever tried it before."

Marco watched as Stella eagerly reached for the Poké Puff. Maddy must have known that Stella would want to be the first to try it. She seemed like the kind of girl who wanted to win at everything.

She took a big bite, and that's when things went crazy. She immediately gagged and spit the cupcake out of her mouth. Maddy shoved a water bottle into her face. And as Stella was gulping down the water, Maddy waved her arm wildly at Marco and Nisha, as if to say, "Run! This is your chance!"

Nisha cracked the door, and Meowth burst out of the cabin. Marco and Nisha followed the cat, racing around the corner.

"Be careful with the mouse!" Nisha whispered as they ran toward the boys' cabins.

"I will," said Marco, cupping Dedenne carefully in his hands. But as he ran, one question kept popping into his head. *What in the world did Maddy put in those cupcakes?* Whatever it was, it had just saved them from getting caught.

CHAPTER TWELVE

"Did you rescue Dedenne?" Maddy rounded the corner of the boys' cabin just seconds after Marco and Nisha.

"Yes!" said Marco. "Here, take him."

Maddy was still carrying the box of Poké Puffs, which she promptly opened and dumped upside down. Two Poké Puffs plopped into the grass below.

As Marco set Dedenne in the box, he heard voices. "Quick. Get inside!" he said to the girls as he pushed open the cabin door.

"But, the rules—" Maddy started to say.

"Forget them," urged Nisha, pulling Maddy in behind her. "I'd rather face Officer Jenny than an angry Stella right now."

Marco couldn't agree more.

As soon as the door was shut, it popped open again. Logan's face was sweaty, as if he'd been running. He didn't seem to care that the girls were standing inside his cabin. "Did you get the mouse?"

"Yes, they rescued him!" said Maddy, stroking Dedenne's head with her finger.

"Good," said Logan. "Where's Sam?"

Marco shrugged. "We haven't seen him yet. I hope Stella isn't punishing him for making her eat that cupcake."

Nisha giggled. "What did you put in there?" she asked Maddy. "Stella looked like she was going to throw up!"

Maddy's eyes twinkled. "A little salt," she said. "Actually, a lot of salt. It was a new flavor I tried just for Stella."

Marco chuckled. Maddy was sweet, sweet, sweet—until someone messed with her mouse. Then look out. "But, wait . . ." he said, remembering. "Officer Jenny almost tried a Poké Puff. What if she'd eaten one of those?"

"I know!" shrieked Maddy. "I thought I was going to die right there on the spot." She shook her head and added, "But I knew Dedenne needed me. I had to be brave and keep going."

"Wait till Stella sees that Dedenne is gone," added Logan, plopping down on his bed. "Then she'll be madder than mad."

"No she won't," said Nisha, smirking.

"Huh?" said Logan. "Why not?"

Nisha grinned. "Because we kind of messed with the crime scene."

She explained how Marco had taken Dedenne out of the box, and she had ripped a hole in the corner and left the box behind.

"It'll look like he chewed his way out?" asked Logan.

"Yeah, and like he is crawling around the room somewhere." Nisha, burst out laughing. "Maybe she'll think he's in her dresser drawers. Or, better yet, she might think he's in the sheets of her bed. Stella won't sleep a wink tonight."

Logan cracked up. "That's genius! But . . . wait. Dedenne is in a box right now. Where did you get that one?"

"It was the Poké Puff box," said Maddy matter-of-factly.

"You dumped another batch of Poké Puffs to put a mouse in there?" asked Logan, his face falling.

Maddy shrugged. "Some of them were a little too salty," she said with a smile.

When someone knocked on the door, they all jumped. Was it Stella looking for revenge?

"It's Sam! Let me in!" came a hoarse whisper.

Logan hopped up to open the door.

"Hey," said Sam, stepping inside. "Nice job with the flute."

Logan looked down at his feet. "Thanks. Nice job with the . . . um, you know. Getting Stella out of the cabin."

Sam nodded.

He looked cheerful, Marco noticed, so Stella must not have been too mean to him. "Hey, Sam," he called. "I've got something for you." He slid the Pokémon trading card out of his back pocket.

"Magnezone!" Sam cried, hurrying over to take the card. He seemed as thrilled to see it as Maddy had been to see Dedenne. "Thanks for getting it back," he said, smiling wide.

"You earned it," said Marco. "We never would have gotten Dedenne back if it wasn't for you."

Sam's cheeks turned pink. "Okay. So I'll see you tomorrow, I guess."

There was a weird silence after that. *Will we be enemies again tomorrow during capture the flag?*

wondered Marco. He had almost forgotten about the game.

As Sam reached for the doorknob, Marco took a step forward. "Wait."

"Yeah?"

"I have something else for you." Marco reached into his front pocket and carefully pulled out the bluish-gray rock.

Sam's eyes darkened when he saw it. "Is that the rock . . . ?"

"Yeah," Marco admitted. "It's the rock I hit you with. I'm really sorry about that. But I was wondering if you . . . if maybe you wanted to have it."

For just a second, Sam looked like his old self. His cheeks got splotchy beneath his bruised forehead. Marco could almost imagine him saying something like, *Why would I want to keep that dumb old rock?*

But Nisha spoke up to help Sam understand. "I think it might be a Samuelite," she said. "It's your Mega Stone, Sam."

"It'll make you stronger," added Maddy. "Like Pokémon who are metavolving."

"Mega Evolving," Nisha corrected her.

Sam reached for the stone and studied it. "A Samuelite?" he said, repeating Nisha's words. "That's kind of cool." He didn't say thanks, but he slid the rock into his pocket. It looked like he was maybe going to keep it for a while.

Marco breathed a sigh of relief.

When Sam was gone, Nisha chewed her fingernail and said, "Remember, guys. Mega Evolution is only temporary."

"You mean, like, Sam might be a bully again tomorrow?" asked Maddy.

Nisha shrugged. "I don't know," she said. "Maybe."

"He's still part of Team Fennekin," Marco pointed out. "That means he kind of has to fight against us."

Logan kicked at the floor. "I was just starting to like him, too. Sort of."

Marco nodded. "Me, too. But at least he has his Mega Stone. He can use it again if he wants to." *And I think he will*, thought Marco. *I don't think Sam is really a bully after all.*

"Here, mighty, mighty Mightyena," called Marco, shading his eyes to search the field. "Where are they all?"

He turned to talk to Pikachu, but the Pokémon wasn't there. Instead, Logan was walking through the grass beside him, wearing his camouflage Balloon Vest.

"Let me at 'em!" said Logan, ready to fight. He took a Mud Ball out of his vest just in case a Mightyena showed up.

Maddy was there, too, carrying a box of Poké Puffs. Marco wondered which ones she had packed today: the sweet ones or the salty ones.

And was Nisha here? He turned around to check, and there she was: walking at the back of the pack. She had some new invention on her head. When she pushed a button, a propeller spun around and lifted her right off the ground. Marco could hear the beep, beep, beep *of the machine as she flew past him.*

He laughed, chasing her. "Wait for me!" he called.

"What's so funny?" asked Logan, who was smacking the alarm clock with his hand. The *beep, beep, beep* finally stopped.

Marco was still lying on his back, laughing. "I'll tell you later," he said. He wanted to wait until all of his friends were together because, for once, they had *all* been in his dream.

After a quick breakfast, Team Treecko was trekking through the woods toward their secret base. That's when Marco told his friends about the dream.

"Usually, I'm attacked by Mightyena in my dreams," he said. "And I can't fight them off. I lose every time. But this time, I couldn't even find a Mightyena to battle."

Nisha laughed when he told her about the propeller hat. "I'll have to start working on that," she said. Then her face grew serious, as if she were actually thinking about a way to make one.

If anyone is smart enough to invent a propeller hat, it's Nisha, thought Marco.

"Hey, I know why you couldn't fight off the Mightyena in your other dreams," Maddy announced.

"Oh, yeah? Why's that?" asked Marco.

"Because you were all by yourself," she said. "We weren't with you."

Marco nodded. "That's probably true," he said. "I didn't have Logan there to beat them up with Mud Balls. And I didn't have any of Nisha's inventions—or your Poké Puffs, Maddy. I don't have any special tricks of my own."

"Sure you do," said Nisha. "You're really good at helping your team come up with a plan."

"Yeah," said Maddy. "You're a good leader."

Marco felt heat rise to his cheeks, so he tried to make a joke. "What type of Pokémon does that make me?" he asked.

Logan tossed a walnut into the air and caught it. "You're not a Pokémon at all," he said simply. "You're a Trainer. You're *our* Trainer."

Huh. Marco liked the sound of that.

When they heard Professor Birch's whistle, they hurried along the trail. It was almost time to start another round of capture the flag. But this time, Marco wasn't nervous.

"It's weird," he said, "but I feel like we already won the game."

Nisha nodded. "I kind of feel like that, too," she said.

"So if we already won," said Logan, "we can just play for fun!" He jogged ahead up the trail and turned around to toss the walnut. "Heads up! Here's the pitch!"

He tossed the walnut to Marco, who caught it one-handed with a smile.